ANNASOPHIA ROBB

Tamra Orr

Mitchell Lane
PUBLISHERS

P.O. Box 196
Hockessin, Delaware 19707
Visit us on the web: www.mitchelllane.com
Comments? email us: mitchelllane@mitchelllane.com

Printing   1   2   3   4   5   6   7   8   9

A Robbie Reader
Contemporary Biography

Abigail Breslin	Albert Pujols	Alex Rodriguez
Aly and AJ	Amanda Bynes	**AnnaSophia Robb**
Ashley Tisdale	Brenda Song	Brittany Murphy
Charles Schulz	Dakota Fanning	Dale Earnhardt Jr.
David Archuleta	Demi Lovato	Donovan McNabb
Drake Bell & Josh Peck	Dr. Seuss	Dwayne "The Rock" Johnson
Dylan & Cole Sprouse	Eli Manning	Emily Osment
Emma Watson	Hilary Duff	Jaden Smith
Jamie Lynn Spears	Jennette McCurdy	Jesse McCartney
Jimmie Johnson	Johnny Gruelle	Jonas Brothers
Jordin Sparks	Justin Bieber	Keke Palmer
Larry Fitzgerald	LeBron James	Mia Hamm
Miley Cyrus	Miranda Cosgrove	Raven-Symoné
Selena Gomez	Shaquille O'Neal	Story of Harley-Davidson
Syd Hoff	Taylor Lautner	Tiki Barber
Tom Brady	Tony Hawk	Victoria Justice

Library of Congress Cataloging-in-Publication Data
Orr, Tamra.
  AnnaSophia Robb / by Tamra Orr.
     p. cm. — (A Robbie reader)
  Includes bibliographical references and index.
  ISBN 978-1-58415-898-1 (library bound)
  1. Robb, AnnaSophia, 1993– —Juvenile literature. 2. Actors—United States—
biography—Juvenile literature. I. Title.
  PN2287.R624O77 2010
  791.430'28092—dc22
  [B]
                                                        2010014898

ABOUT THE AUTHOR: Tamra Orr is the author of more than 250 nonfiction books for readers of all ages, including *Emily Osment* in the Robbie Reader series and more than two dozen other celebrity biographies. Several of her books have won awards, including the New York Public Library Best Nonfiction Book for Teens and Youth Advocates Honorable Mention. Orr lives in the Pacific Northwest with her children, husband, cat, and dog, and in her spare time she reads and watches movies starring the people she has written about.

PUBLISHER'S NOTE: The following story has been thoroughly researched and to the best of our knowledge represents a true story. While every possible effort has been made to ensure accuracy, the publisher will not assume liability for damages caused by inaccuracies in the data, and makes no warranty on the accuracy of the information contained herein. This story has not been authorized or endorsed by AnnaSophia Robb.

TABLE OF CONTENTS

Words in **bold** type can be found in the glossary.

In *Bridge to Terabithia*, AnnaSophia Robb and Josh Hutcherson play best friends. They enter into a magical world that begins in their imaginations.

The Tennis Balls Are Coming!

Leslie looked back over her shoulder. The Hairy Vulture was getting closer every second. She ran as fast as she could. Would she make it? As if being hunted by the Squogres (SKWOH-gurs) was not enough, now she had to deal with danger from the sky! Terabithia (tayr-uh-BIH-thee-uh) was a beautiful place—but a scary one, too.

Although Leslie finally got away in the movie *Bridge to Terabithia*, you could feel her fear as she fought to escape. That was thanks to young actress AnnaSophia Robb. Not only did she have to play the part—she had to look terrified at the same time. If you were being chased by creatures like Squogres, that would be easy. When the producers made the movie, however, Robb was running away from nothing more than her imagination, plus green tennis balls and a man in a blue suit!

Many of the characters in the film were **computer generated** (JEN-uh-ray-ted). Robb had to learn how to act while looking at nothing. "It was a challenge, but it was a good challenge," she said in an interview with Michael J. Lee. "I think just reacting to tennis balls and a man who had a blue suit on was hard for me, but I had seen paintings of all

Not all of the creatures in this fantasy land are friendly, such as the Hairy Vulture.

these mythical Terabithian creatures. So I really tried to **visualize** [VIZH-yool-yz] them when I was acting in the scene."

Robb very much wanted to play Leslie Burke in *Bridge to Terabithia*. She had read the book, and in an interview on *Movies Online* stated, "I remember I would stay up late reading the book and then wake up and start reading again in the morning. It touched me in a way I hadn't been touched by a book before. I really loved the characters and all the **imagination** [ih-maj-ih-NAY-shun]. I think it reminds me that even though I have to grow up, I don't ever have to stop pretending and imagining."

The film also gave Robb a chance to do something different: sing. She lent her voice to the movie's theme song, "Keep Your Mind Wide Open."

Although *Bridge to Terabithia* was not Robb's first acting experience, it was one that she will always remember. She learned a lot, had fun—and found out how to scream at tennis balls!

When Robb arrived at the London **premiere** (preh-MEER) of *Charlie and the Chocolate Factory*, it was hard to believe that she was the same person as she played in the movie.

Chasing a Dream

AnnaSophia Robb was born on December 8, 1993, in Denver, Colorado. She is the only child of David, an **architect** (AR-kih-tekt), and Janet, an **interior designer** (in-TEE-ree-ur dee-ZY-ner). Her parents named her after her Danish great great-grandmother AnnSofie, and her grandmother Anna Marie.

"I wanted to [act] ever since I was really young," AnnaSophia explained in an interview with reporter Nikki Katz. By the time she was eight years old, she had won awards for Irish dancing and had performed in school plays. Her parents found her an agent, and AnnaSophia took an acting class.

David and Janet Robb have always supported AnnaSophia's acting career. When *The Reaping* opened in Los Angeles in 2007, they all showed off proud family smiles.

Her big break did not happen overnight. She went to more than 40 **auditions** (aw-DIH-shunz) before she was hired for a McDonald's **commercial** (kuh-MER-shul). "I don't think I've ever been so excited in my life," she recalled in an interview with *Girls' Life* magazine.

Although she likes being in front of a camera, the job is not always easy. In an interview with *Kidzworld*, she said, "The acting industry is really hard because everyone judges you and looks at you—auditions are so hard because it's [basically] just people staring at you. It's really uncomfortable."

By 2004, she had her first part on television in an **episode** (EH-pih-sohd) called "Number One Fan" for the series *Drake and Josh*. Next she appeared in a television movie called *Samantha: An American Girl Holiday*. For that part, her blond hair was dyed brown. She played an orphan being raised by her wealthy grandmother.

The following year was busy. She modeled fashions for Trad Clothing. She also auditioned to play India Opal Buloni in *Because of Winn-Dixie*. She did not think she would get the role. "I thought I did a horrible job [at the audition]," she admitted to *Girls Incorporated*—but she got the part. The role of Opal was fun. "There are not many characters for kids that have much depth," she said, "and she really has a quality to her. She has an understanding of human beings."

Whether or not she is hired for a part, Robb keeps a good attitude. She told *Girls' Life*, "There are a bunch of different actors, and there are a bunch of different stories. I always look at it like flavors of ice cream or kinds of candy. They might be looking for one kind of candy and you're a different kind, you know?"

Even though she has been in movies with some of the biggest stars, one of Robb's favorite costars is Laiko—better known as Winn-Dixie from the movie *Because of Winn-Dixie.*

Robb walks the runway at a New York City fashion show in 2007. Since the beginning of her career, she has modeled clothing as well as acted.

After these movies, Robb was becoming well known. Her next films would introduce her to more fans.

Stephen Hopkins, director of *The Reaping*, had a table at the 37th annual Comic-Con International Convention. Robb and costar Hilary Swank stopped by to sign autographs and say hello to fans.

Bubblegum Sensation

Over the next few years, Robb was in many different movies. One of her costars, Hilary Swank, said about her, "She is just such a talent. . . . She says so much with her face and with her **expressions** [ek-SPREH-shuns], through her eyes. AnnaSophia is such a joy to work with."

One role that was great fun for her was the gum-chewing, wisecracking Violet Beauregarde in *Charlie and the Chocolate Factory*. This 2005 movie was a remake of *Willy Wonka and the Chocolate Factory*. She kept all the gum she chewed on set, creating a wad the size of a softball. At one point, Violet becomes a blueberry and floats. Robb had to be raised 14 feet into the air. She also had the chance to be a real brat—something she truly enjoyed.

In the film, Robb worked with popular actor Johnny Depp. "He's a really amazing guy . . . ," she reported to *Kidzworld*. "He's just a really sweet man—really normal and loves his kids and is always talking about them."

Although some children think the remake of the movie is scarier than the original, Robb

Playing a gum-chewer like Violet in the movie remake gave Robb other opportunities—like hosting a bubble-blowing contest at Planet Hollywood in 2005.

loved being part of Tim Burton's way of filming. "I think he's the best of everybody. He has such an imagination," Robb said in an interview with Rebecca Murray.

Next, Robb appeared briefly in the film *Jumper*; then she landed leading roles in the **independent** (in-dee-PEN-dunt) films *Have Dreams, Will Travel*; *Sleepwalking*; and *Spy School*. By this time, *Disney Adventure* magazine had named her one of the top sixteen young stars in Hollywood. In 2008, she won Leading Young Actress from the Young Artist Awards.

Since Robb is often on set, she misses large chunks of school. During fifth grade she was homeschooled, but after that she returned to public school. Her teachers work around her absences—and computers help. "With school, everything is online," Robb told reporter Amanda Forr. "I can e-mail my papers. I can e-mail one of my teachers, and they will respond that day. I bring my Mac laptop literally everywhere."

The three stars from *Race to Witch Mountain*, Robb, Dwayne "The Rock" Johnson, and Alexander Ludwig, stop for photographers at the premiere of the movie in 2009.

Keeping It Real

Onscreen, Robb may be a star. At home she is just another kid. She told reporter Paul Fischer, "I still have homework, I still have chores, I still have to wash the toilet in the bathroom. I think that definitely keeps me grounded."

Her next big movie role came as Sara in *Race to Witch Mountain*, costarring Dwayne "The Rock" Johnson. As she told *Crushable*, "I played an alien . . . and I have really cool powers. . . . I can read minds and move objects with my mind." Working with the Rock was fun as well. "Dwayne was amazing," she said to *Just Jared Jr.* "He is such a **genuine** [JEN-yoo-in] guy and so kind and hilarious too! We were always cracking up on the set." She added, "I would love to work with him again."

In 2009, Robb was asked to make the movie *Dear Eleanor* with Abigail Breslin, and the roles kept coming. In 2010, she made *Soul Surfer*, the true story of Hawaiian surfer Bethany Hamilton who lost her left arm in a shark attack at thirteen years old. Brave Bethany returned to surfing and continues to be a top athlete. AnnaSophia also appeared in *The Space Between*, a film about the September 11, 2001, attacks on the United States.

Robb has important advice for other young people who want to be actors. In her *Crushable* profile, she said, "Don't do it because you want to become famous or anything. That was never really my goal. I never saw myself walking down a red carpet or anything. I just thought of performing because I really wanted to be in front of people and performing." She continues, "I think you should make that your goal instead of fame, because

Robb and costar Carrie Underwood walk in the ocean while filming *Soul Surfer*. Robb spent a great deal of time with her arm in a green sleeve. The sleeve makes the arm disappear when filmed against a green screen.

Proving that she really is just like any other kid her age, Robb takes a moment to play a Wii Fit video game.

Robb handles being in the spotlight well—from having her picture taken to signing autographs.

[if it's fame,] then you're not doing it for the right reasons. . . . Be yourself. It's hard with all the **media** [MEE-dee-uh] telling you what you should be (and who you should be). What you do makes you special and that's what makes the world go round—people being different. Just **appreciate** [uh-PREE-shee-ayt] yourself and who you are."

23

Robb's talents as a star have earned her many wonderful opportunities. She has been able to make friends and help people around the world.

To India—And the Future

In between movie roles, AnnaSophia and her family travel. By age fourteen, she had been to many countries, including Mexico, Canada, France, the United Kingdom, New Zealand, and Japan. One of her most memorable trips was to India. She and her friends and family spent two weeks there. They worked with the Dalits, the Untouchables (un-TUT-chuh-buls) of India.

In an essay called "How I Spent My Summer Vacation," she wrote about how the Dalits live: "without proper housing, food and clean water; no education, no political voice, and no chance of escape." The trip truly changed her life. In her paper, she wrote about how she is sponsoring a four-year-old in India. She says, "A little bit goes a long way—it's true. And I sure am glad I went such a long, long way to find that out for myself."

In school, she and fellow classmates have raised money for the people struggling in Darfur, a war-torn region in Africa. She also supports a green company called TerraCycle. This is a group that works to reuse juice packets and other food containers in products like backpacks and school folders.

Robb has big plans for her future. Besides going to college, she says, "I want to do a lot of **nonprofit** [non-PRAH-fit] work, to help people who are less fortunate than I am. I also want to learn more languages."

Dress made of juice pouches

Los Angeles designer Justina Blakeney created a dress made out of Capri Sun juice pouches—with some help from TerraCycle and Capri Sun. Chantellyne Rivera of Miami, Florida, got the chance to model the dress—and to meet Robb—at a special runway event.

In a profile by *Film Monthly*, she said, "I've never really thought of myself as a role model . . . if I continue to make films and my popularity . . . increases, then I definitely have to make the right choices and be a good role model for others. . . . I want to try to help the world."

On her web site, she says, "Show people that you care about them because we really need to start welcoming everybody around us not just our friends and family. We need to start opening up to the world and become one **community** [kuh-MYOO-nih-tee]."

CHRONOLOGY

1993 AnnaSophia Robb is born in Denver, Colorado, on December 8.

2002 She signs with her first agent. She appears in a McDonald's commercial.

2003 She is on an episode of *Drake and Josh*.

2004 She films *Samantha: An American Girl Holiday*.

2005 She films *Because of Winn-Dixie* and *Charlie and the Chocolate Factory*.

2007 She films *Bridge to Terabithia* and *The Reaping*. She travels to India with family and friends.

2008 She films *Have Dream, Will Travel*; *Jumper*; *Sleepwalking*; and *Spy School*. She enters public high school in Denver.

2009 She films *The Space Between* and *Race to Witch Mountain*.

2010 She films *Soul Surfer*.

FILMOGRAPHY

2010 *Soul Surfer*

2009 *Race to Witch Mountain*
The Space Between

2008 *Have Dream, Will Travel*
Jumper
Sleepwalking
Spy School

2007 *Bridge to Terabithia*
The Reaping

2005 *Because of Winn-Dixie*
Charlie and the Chocolate Factory

2004 *Samantha: An American Girl Holiday*

FIND OUT MORE

Books

While there are no other young adult books about AnnaSophia Robb, you may enjoy these other Robbie Reader Biographies from Mitchell Lane Publishers.

Kjelle, Marylou Morano. *Dwayne "The Rock" Johnson*. Hockessin, DE: Mitchell Lane Publishers, 2009.

Mattern, Joanne. *Dakota Fanning*. Hockessin, DE: Mitchell Lane Publishers, 2007.

Mattern, Joanne. *Drake Bell and Josh Peck*. Hockessin, DE: Mitchell Lane Publishers, 2008.

Leavitt, Amie Jane. *Abigail Breslin*. Hockessin, DE: Mitchell Lane Publishers, 2010.

Works Consulted

"AnnaSophia Robb and Alexander Ludwig JJJ Interview." *Just Jared Jr.*, September 1, 2009. http://cnews1.mymostwanted.com/news123/show_news.php?subaction=showfull&id=1251844796&archive=&template=multi-layout-headlines

Beck, Marilyn, and Stacy Jenel Smith. "Garry Marshall Plans AnnaSophia Robb, Abigail Breslin Pic". *Creators.com.*, n.d.. http://www.creators.com/lifestylefeatures/fashion-and-entertainment/hollywood-exclusive/garry-marshall-plans-annasophia-robb-abigail-breslin-pic-why-whoopi-wouldn-t-stay-in-hotel-with-othe.html

Denerstein, Robert. "5 Questions for Annasophia Robb." *Rocky Mountain News*, February 10, 2007. www.rockymountainnews.com/news/2007/Feb/10/5-questions-for-annasophia-robb/

Fischer, Paul. "Annasophia Reaps Her Rewards." *Film Monthly*, February 9, 2007. http://www.filmmonthly.com/Profiles/Articles/AnnaSophiaRobbTerabithia/AnnaSophiaRobbTerabithia.html

Forr, Amanda. "The Secret Life of AnnaSophia Robb." *Girls' Life*, April/May 2009. http://findarticles.com/p/articles/mi_m0IBX/is_5_15/ai_n31484730/?tag=content;col1

Girls Incorporated. "Interview with AnnaSophia Robb." n.d. http://www.girlsinc.org/gc/page.php?id=4.2.30

Katz, Nikki. "AnnaSophia Robb." *Crushable*, August 4, 2009. http://crushable.com/entertainment/exclusive-interview-annasophia-robb/

Lee, Michael J. "AnnaSophia Robb on *Bridge to Terabithia*." Radio Free Network. February 5, 2007. http://www.radiofree.com/profiles/annasophia_robb/interview03.shtml

FIND OUT MORE

Murray, Rebecca. "AnnaSophia Robb Talks About 'Charlie and the Chocolate Factory.'" *About.com Guide to Hollywood Movies*, February 11, 2005. http://movies.about.com/od/charliechocolate/a/charlie021105.htm

Robb, AnnaSophia. "How I Spent My Summer Vacation." Revised November 12, 2008. http://www.annasophiarobb.com/summer_vacation_india.pdf

Roberts, Sheila. "AnnaSophia Robb Interview, *The Reaping*." *Movies Online*, n.d. http://www.moviesonline.ca/movienews_11623.html

Sells, Mark. "AnnaSophia Robb." *The Reel Deal*, March 2008. http://www.oregonherald.com/reviews/mark-sells/interviews/annasophia_robb.html

Sindy. "AnnaSophia Robb Interview." *Kidzworld*, n.d. http://www.kidzworld.com/article/7538-annasophia-robb-interview

Trad Models. "AnnaSophia Robb." *Trad Clothing.com*, n.d. http://tradclothing.com/OurModels.html

On the Internet

AnnaSophia Robb's Official Web Site
http://www.annasophiarobb.com/

TerraCycle
http://www.terracycle.net/

GLOSSARY

appreciate (uh-PREE-shee-ayt)—To value or admire.

architect (AR-kih-tekt)—Someone who designs and draws plans for buildings.

audition (aw-DIH-shun)—A tryout for a part in a play or movie.

commercial (kuh-MER-shul)—An advertisement on TV or radio.

community (kuh-MYOO-nih-tee)—A group of people who work together.

computer generated (JEN-uh-ray-ted)—Usually in movies, characters or scenes that are made using computer programs.

episode (EH-pih-sohd)—One part, or show, in a series.

expression (ek-SPREH-shun)—A show of feelings.

genuine (JEN-yoo-in)—True, honest.

imagination (ih-maj-ih-NAY-shun)—Part of a person's thoughts that do not happen in real life.

independent (in-dee-PEN-dunt)—Made by a small group of people who are not part of a big company.

interior designer (in-TEE-ree-ur dee-ZY-ner)—Someone who earns money by decorating the inside of buildings including houses.

media (MEE-dee-uh)—Sources of information, such as newspapers, radio, television, and the Internet.

nonprofit (non-PRAH-fit)—A group or business that gives all of the money it earns to causes that help others.

visualize (VIZH-yool-yz)—Seeing in one's mind.

INDEX